THIS WALKER BOOK BELONGS TO:

_____

For **Joshua,**
the archetypical bold boy
~**M.D.**

For **Dish** and **Keith**
~**J.R.**

First published 2001 by Walker Books Ltd
87 Vauxhall Walk, London SE11 5HJ

This edition published 2002

2 3 4 5 6 7 8 9 10

Text © 2001 Malachy Doyle
Illustrations © 2001 Jane Ray

This book has been typeset in
Futura Bold and Binner Poster

Printed in Hong Kong

British Library Cataloguing in Publication
Data: a catalogue record for this book is
available from the British Library

ISBN 0-7445-8937-1

The Bold Boy

written by Malachy Doyle

illustrated by Jane Ray

WALKER BOOKS

AND SUBSIDIARIES

LONDON · BOSTON · SYDNEY

A bold boy

found a pea and he put it
in his nut-brown bag.

Then he did a little dance
and he sang a little song
and off he toddled.

"**W**ould you watch
this pea for me?"
said the bold boy,
handing it to an
old woman.

He did another little dance,
sang another little song
and off he toddled.

The woman put
the pea in a bucket,
to keep it safe for
the bold boy.

But a speckledy hen
came into the kitchen.
She saw the pea and,
quick as a flash, she ate it.

"I've come for my pea," said the bold boy.

"I'm sorry to say it's been eaten,"
said the old woman.

"By whom?" said the bold boy.

"My speckledy hen that's standing there.
She's the one who ate it."

"**Naughty, naughty!**"
cried the bold boy, grabbing a-hold
of the speckledy hen and popping her
into his nut-brown bag. "You ate my pea
so now you're mine, for that's
the law where I come from!"

Then he picked up the bag
and off he toddled.

"**W**ill you keep an eye on my hen for me?" said the bold boy, handing her to an old man in the next village.

Then he did a little dance and he sang a little song and off he toddled.

So the old man made
a pen for the little speckled hen,
and he put her inside.

Piggy came to visit
and he frightened Speckled Hen.

She squeaked and squawked,
she flapped her wings,
and over the hill she flew.

"**W**here's my hen?" said the bold boy.

"Frightened away," said the old man.

"**By whom?**" said the bold boy.

"My curious pig," said the old man.

"**Naughty, naughty!**" cried the bold boy,
popping the pig in his nut-brown bag.

"You're mine, you lump," said he to the pig,

"for that's the law where I come from."

The pig was big, but the boy
was bold and off he jolly
well toddled.

"Would you keep an eye on my pig for me?" he asked a young girl in the next village.

The young girl smiled and said she would.

So he did a little dance and he sang a little song and off he toddled.

The poor old pig was tired,
so he curled up in the stable.
But Donkey didn't want
to have a piggy in his bed.
"Ee-haw, ee-haw," he brayed
in Piggy's earhole.

The sleepy pig was
terrified and scarpered
down the lane.

"**W**here's my pig?" said the bold boy.

"Chased away," said the young girl.

"**By whom?**" said the bold boy.

"My lovely donkey," said the young girl.

"**Naughty, naughty!**" cried the bold boy. "Your donkey's mine now, for that's the law where I come from."

And up he jumped and off he galloped.

The donkey was strong
and its legs were long,
but the young girl's
voice was stronger.

"Stop!"
she hollered, and
the donkey stopped.

The boy flew off
and up and over,
head first into a haystack.

"Naughty!"

The girl came running,
the man came running,
the woman came running,
each of them shouting,

"Naughty!"
"Naughty!"

"**Y**ou're the one who's naughty,
stealing a hen and a pig and a donkey.
Make yourself scarce,
you naughty boy, for **that's**
the law round **here!**"

The bold boy drooped,
he was gloomy, he was glum.
He frowned a mighty frown
and he cast his eyebrows down.

And there,
on the ground,
he spied ...

a pea!

He whooped
and he scooped
and he popped
it in his bag.

Then he did a little dance
and he sang a little song
and off he toddled.

MALACHY DOYLE comes from Ireland and lives in Wales, where he writes stories, looking out at the sea. Every time he writes a new one, he climbs up the hill behind his house. "At the top," he says, "I do a little dance, I sing a little song, and off I toddle, just like the bold boy of this story."

Malachy worked in advertising and was deputy head at a school for children with learning difficulties before becoming a full-time writer. Since then he has produced numerous books for children, including *Jody's Beans* illustrated by Judith Allibone and *Sleepy Pendoodle* illustrated by Julie Vivas.

JANE RAY says of **The Bold Boy**, "This is a bright spring morning of a story, when everything is possible. It seems to me to hold something of the very essence of childhood."

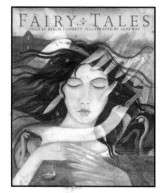

Jane is one of the most acclaimed contemporary children's book illustrators. She has been shortlisted three times for the Kate Greenaway Medal and her many remarkable books include *Fairy Tales* by Berlie Doherty and her own retelling of *Hansel and Gretel*. Jane lives in north London.